Tiger
AND THE
New Baby

For Sam

KINGFISHER
An imprint of Kingfisher Publications Plc
New Penderel House, 283-288 High Holborn
London WC1V 7HZ
First published by Kingfisher 1999

2 4 6 8 10 9 7 5 3 1
1(1TR)/0399/SC/PW/NYM150

Text copyright © Vivian French 1999
Illustrations copyright © Rebecca Elgar 1999

A CIP catalogue record for this book
is available from the British Library.

ISBN 0 7534 0341 2

Printed in Hong Kong/China

Tiger
AND THE
New Baby

Vivian French
& Rebecca Elgar

KING*f*ISHER

"Hello, young Tiger," said Grandpa. "Are you going to show me your new sister?"

"No," said Tiger. "I've got a new train. Look! WOO–WOO!"

Grandpa went to look
at the baby.
"Isn't she lovely?" he said.

"No," said Tiger.
"She keeps crying."

He made his train fall over.
"WOO–WOO! CRASH!"

"Tiger," said Mother Tiger.
"Why don't you show
Tiny your train?"

"What for?" said Tiger.
"She's got her own toys."

He zoomed his train
under the table.
"ZOOM! ZOOM! ZOOM!"

"But Tiny's too little to play on her own," said Father Tiger.

Tiger stayed under the table.

"She's too little to do ANYTHING!" he said. "GRRR!"

Tiny began to cry.

"Why don't YOU play with Tiny's toys?" said Father Tiger. "She can watch."

"Oh," said Tiger. "All right." He crawled out.

All Aboard! WOO-WOO!

Tiger squashed a giraffe,
a bunny and a bear
into the train's trucks.
"WOO–WOO–WOO!"

Tiny stopped crying.

"Goodness!" said Grandpa.
"It won't be long before
Tiny's big enough to play."

Tiger stopped playing.

"Big?" he said.
"How will she be big?"

"Well, Tiny will soon
grow into a great big girl!"
Grandpa told him.

Tiger stared.

Tiger grabbed his train
and twitched his tail.
He turned his back and
stamped upstairs.

"Tiger!" said Father Tiger. "What's the matter?"

"When Tiny grows into a great big girl she'll take away my toys," Tiger said.

Father Tiger gave Tiger a hug. "But you'll grow too," he said. "You'll always be bigger than Tiny."

"Will I?" said Tiger.

Tiger went to look at Tiny.

Tiny looked at Tiger.

"Hello," Tiger said.
"I'm your big brother.
I'll show you how to play."

And Tiny smiled and purred for the very first time.

purr! purr!